Dear Parents,

Welcome to the Scholastic Reader series. We have taken over 80 years of experience with teachers, parents, and children and put it into a program that is designed to match your child's interests and skills.

Level 1—Short sentences and stories made up of words kids can sound out using their phonics skills and words that are important to remember.

Level 2—Longer sentences and stories with words kids need to know and new "big" words that they will want to know.

Level 3—From sentences to paragraphs to longer stories, these books have large "chunks" of texts and are made up of a rich vocabulary.

Level 4—First chapter books with more words and fewer pictures.

It is important that children learn to read well enough to succeed in school and beyond. Here are ideas for reading this book with your child:

- Look at the book together. Encourage your child to read the title and make a prediction about the story.
- Read the book together. Encourage your child to sound out words when appropriate. When your child struggles, you can help by providing the word.
- Encourage your child to retell the story. This is a great way to check for comprehension.
- Have your child take the fluency test on the last page to check progress.

Scholastic Readers are designed to support your child's efforts to learn how to read at every age and every stage. Enjoy helping your child learn to read and love to read.

—**Francie Alexander**
Chief Education Officer
Scholastic Education

For Uncle Chris,
with thanks to Dave
—J.M.

To Edward Helt
—W.W.

Text copyright © 2006 by Jean Marzollo.
"Toys in the Attic," "Make Believe," and "Silhouettes" from *I Spy* © 1992 by Walter Wick; "Creepy Crawly Cave" from *I Spy Fun House* © 1993 by Walter Wick; "The Secret Note" and "The Ghost in the Attic" from *I Spy Mystery* © 1993 by Walter Wick; "Old-fashioned School," "Levers, Ramps, and Pulleys," and "Mapping" from *I Spy School Days* © 1995 by Walter Wick; "A Blazing Fire" from *I Spy Spooky Night* © 1996 by Walter Wick.

Library of Congress Cataloging-in-Publication Data is available.

ISBN 0-439-73864-4

10 9 8 7 6   07 08 09 10

Printed in the U.S.A.   23
First printing, March 2006

I SPY
A BALLOON

Riddles by Jean Marzollo
Photographs by Walter Wick

Scholastic Reader — Level 1

SCHOLASTIC INC. Cartwheel ·B·O·O·K·S· ®

New York   Toronto   London   Auckland   Sydney
Mexico City   New Delhi   Hong Kong   Buenos Aires

I spy

an egg,

 a marble,

a three,

 a clown's white hat,

and a block with a G.

I spy

a ship,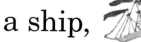

 a multicolored ball,

a cat,

old string,

and A PARASOL.

I spy

a skateboard,

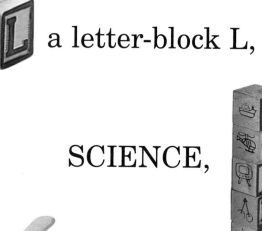 a letter-block L,

SCIENCE,

 a fork,

a balloon,

 and a bell.

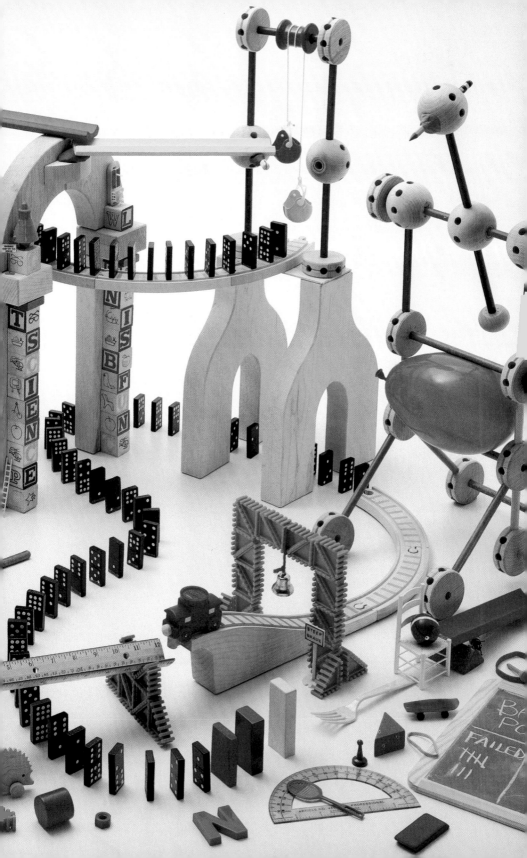

I spy  a deer,

a lonely shoe,

 a giraffe,

a rat,

 and a skeleton, too.

I spy

an elephant,

 a clown's white face,

a rubber band,

and a dress made of lace.

I spy

six snakes,

a scorpion's tail,

a lizard's tongue,

and the shell of a snail.

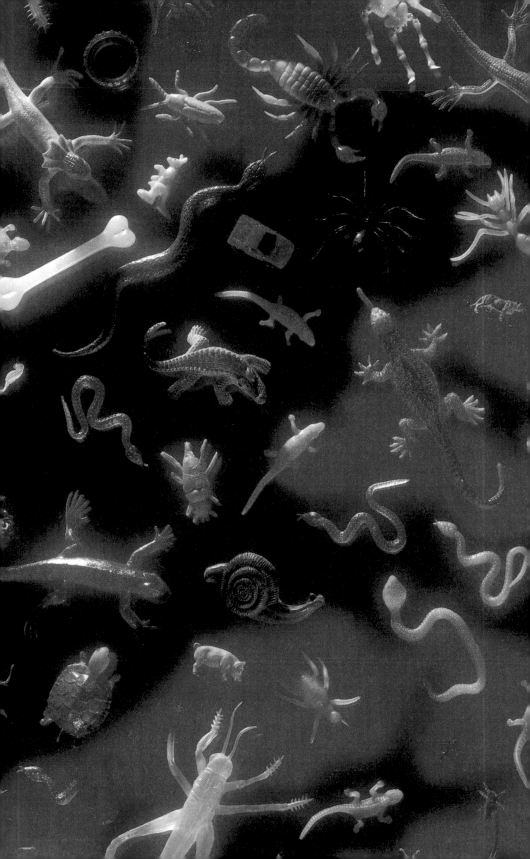

I spy

a plane,

a shovel,

three springs,

a lock,

a crab,

 and a baby with wings.

I spy

a brush,

 a lady on toes,

a spider,

 a ball,

and a bunny in clothes.

I spy

a bench,

 a red fire truck,

a painter,

 a bus,

25,

 and a duck.

I spy  a bottle,

a man with a hat,

 a 2 on a block,

and a tiny black cat.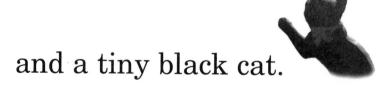

I spy two matching words.

 white hat

white face

bottle

I spy two matching words.

cat

bus

a tiny black cat

I spy two words that start with the letters SK.

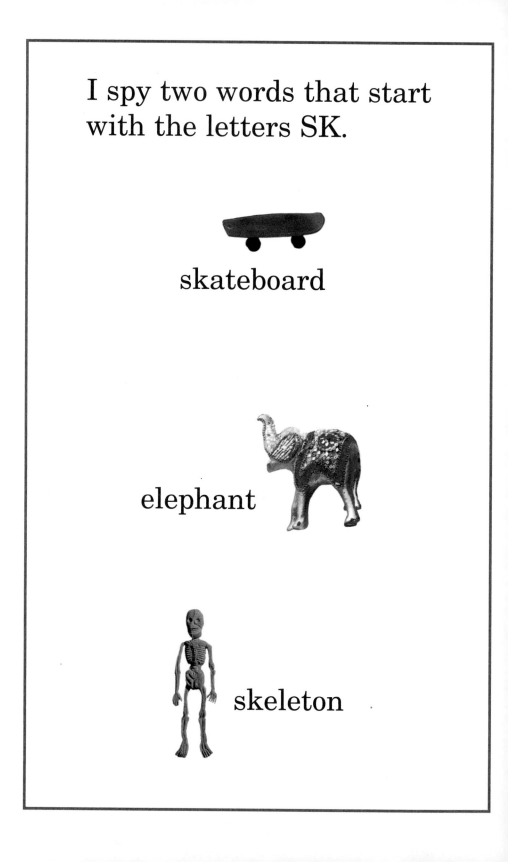

skateboard

elephant

skeleton

I spy two words that rhyme.

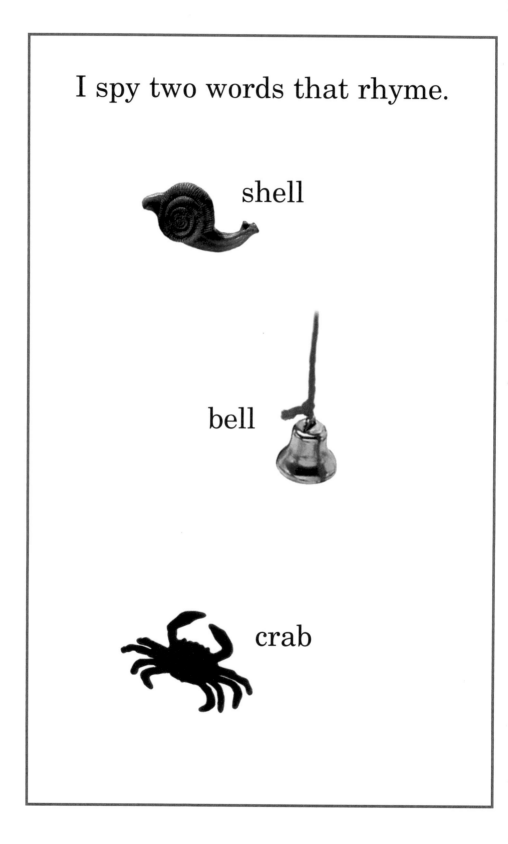

shell

bell

crab

I spy two words that end with an apostrophe plus s ('s).

scorpion's tail

rubber band

lizard's tongue

I spy two words that end
with the letters CK.

lock

brush

block

I spy two words that start with the letters SH.

shovel

shoe

giraffe

I spy two words that rhyme.

egg

rat

hat

Collect all the I Spy Readers!

 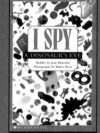  

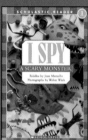 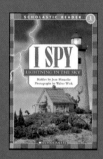 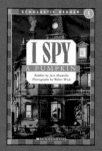 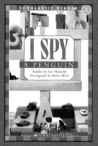

And the original I Spy books, too!

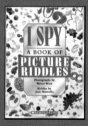 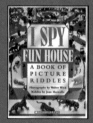 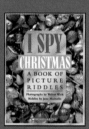

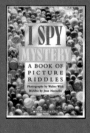 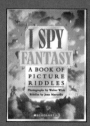 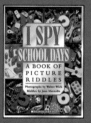 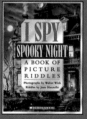 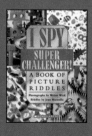

  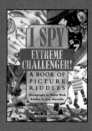